MEETING BILAL

PENGUIN BOOKS

PENGUIN BOOKS

Published by the Penguin Group. Penguin Books Ltd, 27 Wrights Lane, London w8 5tz, England. Penguin Books USA Inc., 375 Hudson Street, New York, New York 10014, USA. Penguin Books Australia Ltd, Ringwood, Victoria, Australia. Penguin Books Canada Ltd, 10 Alcorn Avenue, Toronto, Ontario, Canada m4v 3b2. Penguin Books (NZ) Ltd, 182 – 190 Wairau Road, Auckland 10, New Zealand · Penguin Books Ltd, Registered Offices: Harmondsworth, Middlesex, England · This extract is from *Hideous Kinky* by Esther Freud, first published by Hamish Hamilton Ltd 1992. Published in Penguin Books 1993. This edition published 1996. Copyright © Esther Freud 1992. All rights reserved · The moral right of the author has been asserted · Typeset by Rowland Phototypesetting Ltd, Bury St Edmunds, Suffolk. Printed in England by Clays Ltd, St Ives plc · Except in the United States of America, this book is sold subject to the condition that it shall not, by way of trade or otherwise, be lent, re-sold, hired out, or otherwise circulated without the publisher's prior consent in any form of binding or cover other than that in which it is published and without a similar condition including this condition being imposed on the subsequent purchaser · 10 9 8 7 6 5 4 3 2 1

It was a blue cloudless afternoon and we sat at the front of the crowd in the Djemaa El Fna and watched the Gnaoua dancing. They wore embroidered caps fringed with cowrie shells which tinkled like bells when they moved. They played their tall drums and danced in the square on most afternoons.

'Where do they come from?' I asked Mum.

'They are a Senegalese tribe from West Africa. The King of Morocco has always employed them as his own personal drummers.'

'Because they're so beautiful?' I asked, admiring the elegant wrists and ankles of the dancers as their cymbals rang out in time to the men's drumming hands.

'Maybe.'

Khadija, a plump and solemn-faced beggar girl, wriggled through the crowd and squatted next to me.

'Hello Khadija,' my mother said, noticing her, and Khadija smiled a big gap-toothed grin. She touched my arm and pointed through the crowd across the square to where a group of people were beginning to gather.

'Hadaoui,' she said and began to move towards them, looking over her shoulder to see that I was following.

An old man in faded purple and red robes unfolded a large carpet on which he placed variously shaped brass pots. He filled each one with plastic flowers. He talked to the people who stopped to watch, spreading ripples of laughter through the gathering crowd. Once the carpet was unravelled and every last ornament was in place it became clear not all his comments were directed towards the crowd, but some to a tall, much younger man, who threw his words back at him quietly and with a half-smile that made the people sway with laughter.

The old man sat in the centre of his carpet and blew into a pipe that twisted around inside a bowl of water and bubbled and smoked with each breath.

'What's he doing?' I looked at Khadija and pointed.

'Kif,' she said, hugging her knees and keeping her eyes fixed on the entertainment.

Bea appeared and sat on the other side of Khadija.

'Where's Mum?'

I looked round to see her standing near the young man who was lifting white doves out of a box and placing them on the carpet. The doves ruffled their wings and strutted about, pleased to be in the open.

'Do you think they're going to do any tricks?'

'Who?' Bea said.

'The doves, of course.'

They didn't. It was the old man who did the tricks. He didn't juggle or dance or swallow flaming swords, but somehow, by talking, mumbling, even praying, he held the crowd, grinning and transfixed, straining for his every word. The younger man seemed sometimes to be his loyal assistant and then, disappearing, would emerge on the side of the crowd, heckling and jibing from amongst them, and, just as tempers began to boil, would disclose himself, much to everyone's delight, by leaping into the open and winking slyly all around. Bea, Khadija and I squatted close to the front, with the hard legs of men pressed against our backs.

After the young man had walked twice round the circle on his hands, and the old man had prayed to Allah on a pretend rug, the people seemed to know it was the end. They threw coins on to the carpet and drifted away. I saw my mother throw a coin, but she stayed standing where she was on the other side of the circle.

The Hadaoui's assistant wandered about, stooping now and then to collect the money, which he placed in a leather pouch. He wore sandals and jeans that had once been white and a thin Moroccan shirt with tiny cotton buttons that ran halfway down the front. He had wavy black hair and was taller than Akari the Estate Agent and the other Moroccan men I knew. As the people dispersed, Khadija jumped up and ran on to the carpet where the old man still sat, quietly smoking. She took a red plastic flower from its pot and presented it to the man who was collecting coins. He looked at her for a moment. I held my breath. Then he smiled and bent down to accept it. Khadija ran about under my jealous stare, collecting flowers one by one and standing straight and still to present them, while the assistant, sharing her solemnity, accepted them with a ritual nod of his head. I hovered in my place, envying her bare feet as they padded over the carpet, until, unable to resist a moment longer, I slipped off my plastic sandals and skidded across to join her. The man smiled quizzically as I handed him my first flower. He looked over my head and I saw his eye meet my mother's and so identify me as her child and a foreigner despite my caftan and dusty feet.

Khadija and I watched as the doves were collected one by one and replaced in their cardboard box. 'We've got a pet,' I said to her. 'Not a dove. A hen.' I pointed at the cooing boxes. 'At home. Would you like to see?'

Khadija shook her head, but I could tell she didn't understand. 'Mum, Mum,' I shouted as I ran towards her. 'What's Arabic for hen?' But I stopped before I got there because she was deep in conversation with the magic man's assistant. They were talking in a mixture of French and English and laughing. They turned to me as I ran up.

'There you are,' she said. 'I saw you earlier on, helping Bilal.'

Bilal smiled at me. He had the most beautiful smile of all smiles and his dark eyes twinkled in a face smooth and without a trace of anything unfriendly.

The Hadaoui, Bilal and the white doves stayed in Marrakech for a week, attracting a large crowd every afternoon. Each day Khadija and I waited impatiently for the entertainment to end so we could take up our important role as official helpers to Bilal. The old man remained forever too full of mystery and magic to approach. I kept to the edges of the carpet and avoided meeting his eye.

'When you're old, will you turn into the Hadaoui?' I asked Bilal on the afternoon of his last performance.

'I am the Hadaoui. Now. You don't believe me?' he said in his funny broken English.

'But you're not magic,' Bea said.

'And you don't have a beard.'

Bilal laughed. 'Maybe children can tell about these things. Today the Hadaoui stops here. And from tomorrow I am working as a builder.'

'Here? Staying here?'

'Yes. The Hadaoui must have a holiday. So I become a builder. Here in Marrakech.'

I looked over at Mum to see if she was as excited as me that Bilal wasn't to be going away. She was smiling, but she looked as if she might have known all along.

Bilal came to live with us in the Mellah. Every morning he went out early to work on a building site. In the afternoons when it was too hot to work he took us to the square. Best of all he liked to watch the acrobats. There were a troupe of boys, all about seven or eight years old, dressed in red and green silk like little dragons, who did double somersaults from a standing position and tricks so daring the people gasped and clapped and threw coins into a hat. Bilal instructed us to watch them very carefully.

One day over lunch in our cool tiled kitchen Bilal revealed his plan. 'We will have our own show in the Djemaa El Fna!' he declared triumphantly. Bilal was to be Ring Master. Mum was to make the costumes from silk on the sewing-machine we'd brought with us from England, and Bea and I would be the star guests, performing acrobatic tricks. 'People will love to see the English children do the tricks.' Bilal's eyes sparkled. 'We will have a crowd as big as the Hadaoui and we will collect many coins.'

'But I can't do any tricks,' I said, frightened of diminishing his enthusiasm, but unable to restrain my anxiety.

'Bea, can you do any tricks? At all?'

Bea shook her head. 'I can do a handstand.'

Bilal was undeterred. 'I train you. We start today. Very soon you will be doing this.' He demonstrated with a backward somersault right there in the kitchen.

That afternoon we dressed in shorts and T-shirts and spread a blanket over the paving-stones. 'Soon,' Bilal said, 'you won't be needing any carpet.'

We started with roly-polies. Head over heels. The names made Bilal laugh. Our attempts to perfect this simple trick did not. My version of a roly-poly was a slow tumble which culminated in a star, as I lay flat on my back, my legs and arms stretched in different directions, staring up at the sky. The best part of it, I thought.

'You must end up on your feet.' Bilal frowned. 'Watch me.' From a standing position Bilal took a couple of quick steps, then, tucking in his head, rolled through the air, his bent back barely touching the ground, and he was upright again. 'You see,' he said. 'A flying rolly-polly.'

We kept working at it. Bilal was patient and encouraging. As part of our training he took us regularly to the square, where we sat and watched the acrobats. For me they had taken on a new majesty. They were tiny and fluid and without fear. They cartwheeled through hoops, formed themselves into pyramids and triple-somersaulted off the top, their bodies bending in half as they flew through the air. I imagined Bea and myself dressed in silk, our hair plaited out of the way, dextrous and skilful, taking a bow to the applauding crowd. We would have so many coins to collect that when we sent enough to Bilal's family in the mountains so that he didn't have to work on the building site any more, there would still be some left over. I took hold of Bilal's hand. 'I promise to practise every day, because . . .' And I felt a rush of excitement as the beginnings of a great plan unravelled in my mind. 'Because I've decided that when I grow up I want to be a tightrope walker. You won't tell anyone, will you?'

Bilal nodded. Bilal was someone I could trust.

That afternoon we walked home through the busy streets. I sat on Bilal's shoulders high up above the crowd and from time to time I asked him to let go of my legs so that I could practise balance.

We began going to the park for our training. Mum thought it would be better to practise acrobatic tricks on grass. As the weeks went by, our bodies didn't turn into the fearless, weightless ones Bilal had hoped they would. Or at least Bea's did a little more than mine, but not enough. We began to spend more and more time playing leapfrog, which anyone could do, or lying on the grass telling stories.

Bilal continued to work on the building site. I realized that in order to be a tightrope walker I didn't necessarily have to be an acrobat. So I kept to my own secret plan and practised balancing whenever I got the chance.

As promised, Bilal took us to visit his family in the mountains. We travelled through a whole day on a bus packed with people and then shared a taxi with a man Bilal knew and was happy to see. We had presents of a large packet of meat and three cones of white sugar for Bilal's mother.

The whole village was waiting to greet us at the end of a narrow track that joined the road. 'They welcome you like a wife,' Bilal whispered as Mum stepped out of the taxi. She was dressed in a swirling blue cloak of material that covered her hair and swathed her body in folds that reached the floor. When she walked she drew up the cloth and let it hang over her shoulder.

Bilal introduced us to his mother. She was a large lady with a throaty voice that billowed out from under her veil. Bilal's father was really an old man and half her size.

The women threw flower petals into the air and sang a low lilting song as we walked back along the path. From 11

time to time they let their fingers brush against my hair.
I held tightly on to my mother's hand.

The village was a cluster of low white houses at the
foot of a hill that was almost a mountain. We followed
Bilal into the dark inside of his family's house. Bilal's
family trooped in after us, and we all stood about
smiling. Bea nudged Mum and she remembered and
handed over the meat and the sugar.

'You see, she likes the presents,' Bilal whispered as
his mother nodded, unwrapping and rewrapping her
gifts. I had tried to convince him that she might prefer
a Tintin book or a clay drum.

That night Mum, Bilal, Bea and I all slept on rugs
in the room that was the house, and Bilal's parents,
his brothers and sisters, their wives and children all
slept outside in the garden. It was a clear warm night
and very light from so many stars.

'I wish we could sleep in the garden too,' I said to
Bea and she agreed.

'Where's Abdul?' Bea asked next morning over break-
fast. We were drinking coffee sweetened with the sugar
we had brought. Abdul was Bilal's youngest brother
and the same age as Bea. We had tried to teach him
12 hopscotch the evening before.

'Abdul goes to look after the sheep,' Bilal said. 'He is up before the sun.'

'Where?' I asked, looking round for even a single sheep.

'On the other side of the mountain.' Bilal pointed into the hazy distance. 'Over there are all the sheep of the village.'

'Are there other people helping?'

'No, just Abdul.'

So Abdul was a shepherd. I had seen a shepherd that wasn't old and frozen and on the front of a Christmas card. By lunchtime he was back from his day's work.

The whole family ate from one enormous bowl. It was couscous with a sauce of seven vegetables. I tried to copy the exact movement of Bilal's hand as he collected the tiny grains of couscous in the crook of his finger, swept them into a ball with his thumb, and placed it in his mouth without a crumb being spilt or wasted.

'Tomorrow can I go to the mountains with Abdul?' I asked him when the meal was over.

Bilal shook his head. 'No. Because tomorrow we are going to the festival of the marabouts.'

The festival was a little like a market.

'What's a marabout?' I wanted to know.

Mum pointed out a small white building with a domed roof and a bolt on the door. 'Marabouts are holy men, like saints, who live in these little houses.'

'Is he in there now?'

Mum wasn't sure. She asked Bilal.

'Oh yes. He's in there.'

'Will he come out once the festival starts?'

Bilal looked amused. 'No. It is only his spirit we celebrate.'

We walked towards the building. I peered on tiptoe over the white wall surrounding it.

'For many years,' Bilal said, 'he is lying dead inside.'

Mum and I both pulled away.

Bilal's brothers were erecting a large white tent. It was a tent like others that were going up around the edges of the festival. Round and cool inside. The women from each section of the family were laying out rugs and cotton spreads of material to sleep on. They sat and talked from under their veils while their smallest children slept.

'They wanted Mum to wear a veil,' Bea whispered. 'Who did?'

'The mother and the brothers and everyone else.'

'Why didn't she then?'

'She said she wouldn't.'

'Are they angry?' I looked over at the women resting, their eyes sharp above a square of black.

'It's hard to tell,' Bea said.

If you stood very close to the veil you could see through the black and tell whether someone was wearing lipstick or not. I wondered if it was a special magic cloth.

'Nylon,' Mum said when I asked her.

When I woke, Ahmed had arrived. Ahmed was Bilal's brother-in-law.

'Ahmed is married to Bilal's sister,' Mum explained.

'No,' Bilal corrected her. 'Ahmed is divorced from my sister.'

Ahmed had two other wives with him and several children. They spread out their belongings near to ours and the youngest wife tried to settle her baby who was crying. As she wrestled with her child, her veil floated up and I saw her face. She was pale and looked a little like Bilal's sister Fatima who was fourteen and wearing a veil for the first time.

The baby kept on crying. Ahmed's other wife took it from her and began to walk around the tent, rocking and soothing it with words.

Bea and I wandered out into the warm night. The circle of white tents had grown, stretching away round the marabout's shrine. Outside each tent fires were burning and meat roasted on twisting sticks. Ahmed, Bilal and Mum sat by our fire. They were smoking a clay pipe. Passing it from one to another in a circle.

Ahmed began to sing. His voice was sad. He sang the Egyptian songs that played in the outdoor cafés in Marrakech. His voice rose and fell and caught in his throat with such pure sorrow that I was surprised not to see tears running down his face. Bilal joined in on a lower note with a smile on his lips as if to say it wasn't his sad story he was singing.

I crawled on to Mum's lap and basked in the melancholy music and the warmth of the fire. The sour smell from the burning pipe mingled with the roasting meat turning on its spit. It looked like a sheep and I wondered whether or not it was one of Abdul's. If it was, I decided, thinking of Snowy, I would refuse to eat it. Much later that night, when the singing had spread from tent to tent and supper was finally ready, I forgot about my earlier resolutions and, along with Abdul, held out my hands for a kebab.

Mum washed my feet and hands in a bowl of cold water and insisted I change into my nightie. Abdul and his cousins were sleeping where they'd fallen, wrapped tight in their djellabas.

'Can I have some powder on my feet, please?' I asked, as much to keep Mum in the tent as to feel it, silky smooth between my toes.

She took a tin of Johnson's Baby Powder out of her bag and sprinkled me a ration. Ahmed's youngest wife, still rocking her tireless baby, watched us darkly from behind her veil. As I patted each toe dry, she laid her baby down and slowly unwrapped its clothes, revealing a damp red ring around its neck. Mum leant over and offered her the tin. She stared uncomprehendingly, until Mum shook a fine layer of white on to the baby's neck. She smoothed it gently and the crying seemed to quiet a little. The lady held on to Mum's hand. 'Thank you, thank you,' she said in Arabic.

Mum pressed the tin into the woman's hands. 'Sprinkle a little every day,' she said, pointing at the baby.

'What about me?' I hissed at her.

17

'Shh.'

'But it's our only tin.'

Mum glared.

I put my head under the blanket. 'I want Bilal,' I wailed. When I refused to come out even to kiss her goodnight she relented a little and promised to ask Linda to bring some powder with her when she came to visit.

'When will that be?' I asked.

Mum tucked me in and sneaked a butterfly kiss that tickled before going out to rejoin the party.

'Who's Linda, anyway?' I asked Bea, when she eventually came to bed.

'You know . . . Linda,' Bea said.

'Linda?'

But Bea said she'd only tell me if I told her a story first and by the time I'd finished 'The Adventures of a Spooky Carpet' she was asleep.

There was everything for sale at the festival. Donkey-loads of water melons, pomegranates, blood oranges – the insides of which you could suck out through a hole in the skin. There was a stall with hundreds of pairs of babouches, the softest most beautiful shoes. They were mostly in yellow or light brown leather but some were black and patterned with stars of silver or gold. There was one pair, red with a zigzag of green, the toes of which curled up like magicians' slippers, that made my eyes burn with wanting them. I was frightened to pick them up or even touch them, and the old man who sat among his slippers gave me no smile of encouragement.

'If you could have any babouches you wanted in the whole world, which ones would you choose?' I asked Mum.

She bent down to finger the leather. 'I was thinking of making you and Bea some sandals . . .' she said.

My heart fell.

'Out of leather. With rubber soles. They'll be very nice.'

'But they won't be like these.'

'No, they won't be quite like these,' she said, and she drew me away.

By that evening news of Mum's miracles with the baby powder had spread throughout the tent.

'Oh yes, she is the wise woman from the West,' Bilal said proudly, and he put his arm around her.

'There is a lady Ahmed wants you to help,' Bilal told Mum on our last night around the fire. Ahmed 19 had been particularly impressed by the baby-powder cure. 'He has invited us to visit with him.'

The white tent came fluttering down. We said goodbye to Bilal's family who we would see again in a few days, and to Fatima, who was my favourite sister, and Abdul. We set off in a different direction with Ahmed and his two wives and their children. The baby's rash had almost vanished, but it still screamed unceasingly. No one took the slightest bit of notice.

During our journey on a bus crowded with people who had all been at the festival, Ahmed explained through Bilal what he wanted Mum to do. 'There is an aunt of Ahmed,' he said, 'who is sad because she has lost her favourite nephew in a car crash. Since he is dead she will not be happy to live.'

'But what does he want me to do?' Mum asked.

Bilal didn't translate her doubts to Ahmed. 'Just talk with her,' he said, smiling assuredly. 'Just visit and talk with her.'

The old lady lived in a room at the back of Ahmed's house, which was large and airy with tiled floors and slatted shutters covering the windows, filtering in just enough light to see. Ahmed wanted Mum to go to her

right away.

'I want to come too,' I said. I wouldn't let go of her hand. I couldn't let go. She mustn't go alone into a dark room with a woman who wanted to die, I thought. She might never come out again.

'Stay with the women,' Mum ordered.

I looked over at the silent veiled wives who waited for me, and my breath caught in my throat. 'Please,' I appealed, my voice wild. 'Bilal, tell her please.'

Mum stood unsure. I could feel her staring at me. 'It's just that they're tired,' she said, and we all walked in silence round to the back of the house.

The old lady was lying in her bed when Ahmed ushered us into the room. Startled by the light, she sat up. Her face was striped with thin lines of dried black blood where she had dragged her nails hard across it. My mother sat on the edge of the bed and rummaged in her bag. She pulled out a large bound book. It was her copy of the *I Ching*. She undid the twist in the velvet pouch Bilal had made for her and poured the three large coins into her hand, warming them in her palm as she always did before she told a fortune. Ahmed's aunt watched her with a glimmer of light in her yellow eyes. Mum handed her the coins. They were Arabic coins with stars on one side and the head of the King on the other.

'I want you to throw the coins for me,' Mum said. Bilal spoke to the aunt softly in Arabic and she scattered the three coins on to the bedspread with a thin worn hand.

Mum made a line in pencil in the back of the book and nodded for her to throw again. The old lady threw the coins six times and Mum made a pattern of six broken and unbroken lines, three on each side of a space.

Mum opened the book. The old lady was sitting a little straighter with her shawl held tightly around her shoulders. Mum began to read. 'Persistence brings good fortune. It will be of advantage to cross the great river. The Superior Man will pass this time in feasting and enjoyment . . .' Bilal translated in a low murmur as she read and the old lady blinked in concentration with her head slightly on one side. Mum read on and on about lakes and rivers and turning-points until my mind began to wander away from the room.

'Do you think we'll get a chapter of *Bluebeard* tonight?' I whispered.

'Shhh.'

'We haven't had any story for ages.'

The reading was over. There was a silence. Then the old lady smiled and, looking towards Ahmed, commanded him in a startlingly strong voice to bring mint tea and bread. Ahmed hurried out like a small boy. I could hear him shouting out the order as he ran through the house.

Once she had drunk a glass of tea and chewed at the soft inside of a roll, the old lady pushed back the covers and began to climb out of bed. Ahmed smiled a tender smile as her narrow feet touched the floor. She walked slowly over to a painted chest which stood under the window and, opening it, took out a sky-blue caftan. She reached up and held it against my mother's shoulders.

'Thank you,' my mother said, taking it from her.

With the faintest of smiles the old lady climbed back into bed and motioned for us all to go away.

It was mid-morning when we arrived back in Bilal's village. I could see Fatima standing in the doorway of her father's house. I waved and began to run towards her, but instead of coming to meet us she turned and darted inside letting the curtain fall across the door.

'Fatima,' Bilal called after her. 'Fatima,' he ordered, and she reappeared, limping slightly and with a split across her lip.

'What happened to you?' Mum gasped, but Bilal 23

took his sister roughly by the shoulders and began to question her in a voice which shook with anger. Fatima spoke a few tearful words with her head bowed and her eyes on the ground.

'What's happened?'

'It's nothing,' Bilal said. 'Let's get inside.'

The familiar cool of the house had turned so cold it made me shiver. Finally Bilal spoke. 'It is important that Fatima will not make bad her reputation. If she is not good, she will not be married.'

Mum was silent. She looked at him with cold, accusing eyes.

'Fatima has behaved very badly at the festival,' he said.

'Yes?'

'She was seen without her veil – watching the dancing. At night she must stay inside the tent.'

'So she was beaten,' Mum said flatly.

I looked over at Fatima, huddled in the corner, her fingers moving through a bowl of string beans.

'My brothers tied her in the barn and beat her . . .' Bilal looked away, ashamed, then added, 'But now she will be good and then she will be married.'

Fatima lifted the bowl in her arms and hobbled silently to the back door.

Mum watched her go. 'I think maybe it's time to go home,' she said.

'Tomorrow,' Bilal insisted. 'Stay until tomorrow and we will all go back to the Mellah.'

Bilal could not find any work in Marrakech. The Hadaoui was still on holiday and our money had not arrived at the bank. 'I have friends in Casablanca who have work,' he said, 'they are expecting me.'

'Casablanca. Where's that? Can I come?'

'I'll come back and visit.' Bilal knelt down so I could climb on to his back. I clung to him as he wandered around the house gathering up his things.

Bilal left with one half-empty bag, dressed in the same faded clothes I'd first seen him in. We stood by the garden wall and waved to him until he disappeared.

That night we ate supper in the kitchen. We didn't go out to the square as we usually did. No one even mentioned going.

'If our money doesn't come this week,' Mum said, 'we'll have to move.'

'What'll happen to Snowy if we move?' Bea's voice was a challenge.

'We'll take her with us,' Mum soothed, but absentmindedly. She lit the paraffin lamp with a twist of paper.

'Couldn't you make Akari's little girl another dress?' I asked.

Mum didn't think so.

A week later we moved into the Hotel Moulay Idriss. It stood in a narrow street behind the Djemaa El Fna and was built around a courtyard of multipatterned tiles in the centre of which grew a banana tree that was taller than the top floor. Snowy would have loved to play among the tree roots and make dust baths in the earth, but the only room they had to offer was on the second floor. It was a large room with two doors that looked out on to the courtyard and no window. We brought our mattresses from the Mellah to sit and sleep on and Mum set up a kitchen in one corner with the mijmar. The leaves from the banana tree cast a soft green shadow.

Bea made a nest for Snowy with straw. She encouraged her to sit in it and maybe even lay an egg, but Snowy wanted to explore. She set off at a run along the landing that linked the rooms on all four sides of the hotel.

'All right, I'll train her to find her own way home.' And Bea scattered liberal handfuls of corn over both 27 our doorsteps. Snowy liked the Hotel Moulay Idriss. Soon she was striding about with confidence, clucking and pecking her way into other people's rooms and leaving little piles of yellow-white droppings wherever she went.

Next door lived a family with five children, and a grandmother who slooshed down her stretch of landing first thing each morning with water from a metal bucket. Each time Snowy dared to pass her by, she hissed and shooed and flicked the ground with the edge of her djellaba.

Once the corridor was dry, a girl, not much taller than Bea, appeared. She stood patiently on the landing to be checked over by the fierce old lady. Her hair was braided into two plaits and she wore a white pleated skirt and sandals. Over one shoulder she carried a leather satchel.

'Where's she going?' Bea asked.

'Who?' Mum said sleepily.

'The girl next door. Come and look.'

'I expect she's just going to school.' Mum stretched out under the covers and then in a coaxing voice she said, 'If you make some strong tea with sugar in, I'll get up. I promise.'

The next morning we were woken by the lady who lived in the room on our other side. She stood in the doorway and shouted, loud enough to wake the whole hotel. She held a dark red sequinned cushion in one hand, carefully like a tray, on which was a murky yellow stain. She pointed an accusing finger at Snowy who sat innocently in her nest of straw, chattering happily, her feathers up around her neck. The woman stood there, holding out her cushion and shouting. Mum struggled out of bed and tried to reason with her, but the woman continued to point at the cushion, at Bea, and at herself, and then with a vicious kick in Snowy's direction she swept out of the room. Bea rushed over and picked Snowy up in her arms. Her eyes were spinning with alarm. The woman's shouts of fury continued through the dividing wall.

Mum sat on the end of Bea's bed. 'It looks like we're going to have to find Snowy another home.'

Bea didn't answer. Then she said in a very small voice, 'I'll train her.'

'I'll talk to Akari,' Mum said. 'He'll know what to do.'

That afternoon Akari came and took Snowy away.

'I will look after her. Very special,' he beamed as he hurried down the corner stairs.

We refused to return his smile. 'Like hell,' Bea said under her breath.

The only people who commiserated with us on the loss of our pet were the two women who lived on the opposite side of the landing. When they saw Akari disappear down the stairs with Snowy clucking her last in a cardboard box, they came across and offered Mum Turkish cigarettes and a glass of wine. They were big women who wore brightly coloured djellabas with silky hoods halfway down their backs, and their hands and feet were covered in an intricate web of design.

'Tattoos,' Bea whispered.

'Henna,' the woman nearest me laughed, noticing my fascinated stare. She took my face and held it still with one hand, while with the fingers of the other she twisted a strand of my hair between her fingers. It made a dry, brittle sound in her hand like the scratching of an insect. 'Henna,' she said, turning to Mum and switching to French to convince her.

'They say you need henna on your hair to make it grow thick and long.'

I looked at their heavy plaits.

'All right,' I agreed.

I was taken through the curtain into the dark recess of their room. It smelt of perfume and night-time, as if they had lived in it for ever. Bea was sent to get a towel and to fill a bucket from the tap in the corner of the courtyard. My hair was brushed back off my face in preparation.

The women poured a heap of green powder into a bowl and, with Bea's water, stirred it into a thick mud that smelt like mud but with something sweet and something sour mixed in. They patted the henna, cold and slimy, into every strand of my hair, coiling it up on top of my head, so that when they'd finished I felt like I was wearing a soft clay helmet. They dipped the corner of the towel in water and wiped away the streaks of green from my face and ears.

I was led triumphantly back on to the balcony, where Mum was still sipping wine in the sun. She laughed when she saw me.

'Isn't Bea going to have her hair hennaed too?' I asked, desperate suddenly not to be the only one, the only experiment. The women smiled, and as sharply as if I had ordered it they took her inside.

Soon Bea and I were both sitting in the sun, weighed down and sleepy with the mud cakes drying on our heads. We had resigned ourselves to a long, hot day 31 on the terrace of the Hotel Moulay Idriss, watching the comings and goings of the various inhabitants and from time to time catching a glimpse of Moulay Idriss himself when he emerged from the gloom of his office on the ground floor.

'Can I take it off now?' I asked Mum, once she had started to prepare the evening meal, but she shook her head and said, 'It would be best to keep it on until tomorrow morning.'

I began to protest.

'That's what the Ladies said. If you keep it on until the morning, your hair will grow thicker and longer than anyone else's.'

'The morning!'

I sat against the wall between the doors of our room, playing with Mum's box of buttons and beads, thoughts of Rapunzel dancing through my mind, and wondered how I'd be able to get to sleep that night.

The next morning when I tapped at the top of my head it echoed like a clay drum. Mum sent us round to the Ladies to have the henna taken off. The hardest
pieces were cracked away, catching and pulling at

strands of baked hair, and the rest was soaked out in a bowl of water. The water, when I looked at it, was a dark, steamy red that grew thinner and paler with every rinse. When the water was clear and my hair had been combed straight down on either side of my face, I was sent outside to look at myself in a tiny round mirror.

At first I thought it must only be a reflection of the sun beating down through the banana leaves, but once I'd pulled my hair around in front of my eyes, I was not so sure. I looked at it hard, then again in the mirror, then attempted to match up the two colours, which were in fact one colour. The colour of my hair. Orange.

Still clutching the mirror, I ran along the landing to find Mum.

'Look. They've tricked me,' I sobbed, throwing myself down on the floor. 'It's horrible. I hate it. And I hate them.' And I hate you, I added to myself, for conspiring in this master trick against me.

Mum knelt down and lifted up my face. She pushed the still-damp hair out of my eyes. 'It's beautiful,' she soothed. 'Beautiful. It's a rich dark red, it's copper, it's auburn . . .'

'It's orange,' I wept.

'Haven't you noticed,' she continued, 'all the most 33

beautiful girls in Marrakech have hennaed hair?'

I shook my head.

'You haven't noticed? I'll take you for a walk and show you.'

Just then Bea appeared in the doorway. She was a dark shadow in a blazing halo of red and gold.

'What do you think?' she said.

The sun behind her picked out a thousand colours in her hair and set them flying against one another like the fighting flames of a torch.

'It's beautiful,' Mum and I both said in one breath and she squeezed me tight in spite of myself.

'Will you run and bring our towel back,' Mum asked Bea, as we were about to leave for the square. 'And take the Ladies' mirror . . . and say thank you,' she shouted after her.

We waited in the courtyard. I had tucked all my hateful hair up inside a hat in the shape of a fez. It was a hat made from cotton covered in tiny holes for cross-stitch, which Bilal had embroidered pink and green before he left for Casablanca. I was hot and I felt Mum's scornful eye on me.

'Come on,' she grumbled.

Finally Bea appeared. 'They won't give it back,' she said.

'What do you mean?'

'The towel. It was hanging in their room but when I tried to take it, they said it belonged to them.'

Mum laughed and looked up at their landing. The curtain hung heavily across the entrance to their room, and even though we waited neither one nor the other appeared.

The square was very busy. We sat outside a café while Mum drank black coffee and Bea and I sucked warm Fanta through a straw. It was unbearably hot under my hat. Little streams of sweat fell down around my ears and into my eyes, but it had been too big a fight to get the hat on to enable me to take it off. I sweated and suffered.

There was a man selling majoun on the corner. He was not always there. Mum bought a piece like a little chunk of rock. She let us both break off a sliver with our teeth. It tasted delicious, like crystallized sugar with soft honeycomb that hid something sharp that made you want more to cover the trace of bitterness.

'Please can we have a piece? Please?' we begged, forced on by the delicious sweetness of it.

'It's not meant for children. It'll make you . . .' – she was searching for the word – 'drunk.'

'Please, please,' we insisted. 'Majoun, majoun, majoun,' and we set up a chant rising in volume with every refrain.

'Shhh,' Mum tried to quiet us, frantic, but giggling

herself. 'All right, you can share a piece, but for God's sake be quiet about it.'

We handed over our dirham and pointed and whispered, 'Majoun,' as we had seen it done. We were handed a twist of newspaper inside which was small lump of hashish pounded into a sweet like fudge. We sat at the table and took turns scraping fragments off with our teeth. It seemed to me the most delicious taste in the world. Sand mixed with honey and fried in a vat of doughnuts. We passed it back and forth, giggling a conspiracy of joy and adventure.

'Let's make it last for ever,' I said, barely touching it with the tip of my tongue.

'Let's go and see if Luigi Mancini's in town.' Bea slid off her chair.

I glanced at Mum. 'We'll meet back here,' she said.

Looking for Luigi Mancini had become our favourite game. We investigated one café at a time, reporting to each other the movements of any tall man dressed in white. Sometimes we would settle on a particularly suspicious Luigi Mancini look-alike and follow him through his afternoon's business.

'Don't forget,' Bea would say, 'he might have dyed

his hair, shaved off his moustache, or given up smoking.'

Today, light-headed and bursting with laughter, it was hard to remain unnoticed by anyone. We crept up staircases, across terraces and around the tables of the largest cafés, whispering 'Luigi Mancini' almost inaudibly, and then standing like statues to monitor the reaction.

Today there was no one who could possibly be mistaken for Luigi Mancini, or even Luigi Mancini's brother. There was no one in the café who was not Moroccan.

Then I heard a woman's voice. 'Excuse me, hello, can anyone speak English? Hello?'

'Listen.' I pulled at Bea's sleeve.

Then we both heard it.

'Hello, do you speak ENGLISH? I'm trying to find . . . oh dear . . .'

'It's Linda,' Bea said.

'Linda?' But she had already darted off in the direction of the small crowd of waiters that had gathered.

Linda stood surrounded by suitcases, a fat and sleeping baby propped on one hip. She was holding out a crumpled scrap of paper.

'Hello, Linda. What are you doing here?' We

squeezed into view between the legs of the onlookers.

Linda sat down on a bulging duffle bag and burst into tears.

'I'll go and get Mum,' Bea said and disappeared.

'What's your baby called?' I asked as she wiped her eyes with toilet paper from a roll.

'Mob,' she said.

'Can I hold it?'

'Her.' She passed the baby over.

As soon as Mob was on my lap she woke up and began to scream.

'Have I met you before?' I asked.

Linda nodded.

'Did you have a baby when I last saw you?' I had to shout over Mob's yells.

'No.'

'How old is she?'

'Six months.'

'Why's she called Mob?'

Linda sighed. 'Because her father was an Anarchist.'

'What's an Anarchist?'

Mum and Bea had arrived. Linda stood up and blew her nose. 'Didn't you get my letter?'

And Mum said, 'Didn't you get mine?'

Then they both began to laugh and hugged each 39

other and we all helped to carry Linda's luggage back to the Hotel Moulay Idriss.

'I bought you a dress with the money you sent.' Linda riffled through her suitcase. 'From Biba.'

We watched as Mum tried it on. It was a soft cotton dress in golden browns and oranges, like a park trampled with autumn leaves. It had bell-shaped sleeves that buttoned at the wrist.

'I love it,' Mum said, spinning around in a dance.

I heaved a private sigh of relief. Surely this meant now she would stop wearing her Muslim haik that turned her into someone's secret wife, with or without a veil.

'You look beautiful.' Linda was still heaping clothes on to the floor.

'Yes, beautiful, beautiful,' I agreed, eager to encourage.

Bea didn't say anything. Her face was set and worried.

'And I bought these for you.' Linda held out a pair of faded black trousers. 'From the Portobello Road.'

I gasped with excitement as I tried them on. They even had a zip.

'Do I look like a boy?'

'Not really.' Mum was rolling up the legs in thick wedges round my ankles.

'I thought she'd have grown . . .' Linda said.

'Not even with my hat?' I looked around for it. In my excitement I had forgotten the horror of my orange hair.

Bea had a striped T-shirt that was long enough to be a dress. It had a hole under one arm.

'Are you Linda who was going to bring the baby powder?' I asked.

Bea jumped up. 'So you did know she was coming. You did know.' She turned on Mum.

'I didn't know exactly when . . .'

Bea's face was dark. 'You should have told me.'

'I'm sorry.' Linda looked as if she were going to cry again.

'Don't be silly.' Mum held Bea at arm's length. 'Everything will be fine. Linda and Mob can stay here. There's plenty of room.'

'There's plenty of room.' Bea mimicked, almost under her breath but loud enough to strangle the air in the room. Mob gurgled in Linda's arms and was sick. Linda mopped it up with toilet roll.

'In the toilets in Morocco they only have a water 41

tap and sometimes they just have stones,' I told her.

Bea walked out on to the landing and hung her head over the railings. It was beginning to grow dark and the grey shadows outside, for a moment, exactly matched the half-light in the room. Mum lit a lamp and Bea disappeared into sudden darkness.

She kicked at the door-frame as she came back in. 'I have to start school,' she said.

Relief clouded my mother's face. 'Of course. Well you can.'

'How can I?' Bea was unimpressed. 'I need a white skirt – which I don't have. I need a white shirt – which I don't have. I need a satchel.' She stood in the middle of the room victorious. 'You see. I can't.'

'Tomorrow first thing we'll go to the bank and see if our money has arrived and if it has we'll buy you a uniform before we do anything else.'

'And if it hasn't?'

'We'll just have to wait a few days.'

'And if it still hasn't?'

'We'll think of something,' Mum promised.

'Will you think of something for me as well?' I asked.

'You don't want to go to school.' Her voice was decisive where it concerned me. 'School is for big girls like Bea and Ayesha next door.'

A few days turned into a few more days and Mum borrowed some money from Linda. We went to the market to choose material. A large piece of white cotton. We left Bea to bargain for it while we waited at the next stall.

'How did she learn to speak Arabic like that?' Linda asked, as Bea haggled over the price.

Mum and I exchanged vague looks. 'She just seemed to pick it up.'

'Bea does all the shopping now,' I told her, 'because she's got brown eyes and mine and Mum's are green.'

'They think she's a little Moroccan girl,' Mum explained. 'We save a lot of money that way.'

Mum sat at home all that day and into the night sewing a pleated skirt and a white shirt with short sleeves. Ayesha was invited into our room so that Mum could inspect her uniform. She brought her schoolbook with her.

'It must be my turn to look at it now,' I whined when it seemed to have gone round the room at least

44

twice. Ayesha watched anxiously as we pored over her book. On the front were two children: a boy and a girl. They were holding hands and about to take a step. The girl had a bright yellow dress against a red background and the boy was red on yellow. They both had short black hair. On the first page there were pictures of animals in different coloured squares.

'Wasp, bat, ant, crocodile.' I held my breath for a scorpion.

'You're meant to say them in Arabic, stupid.' Bea started to rattle through the animals. She had a little help from Ayesha. Tortoise, for example. There were pages and pages of animals and objects of every kind. Telephones, syringes, shoes. All in coloured boxes and some of them had black squiggles above.

'What's this?' I pointed to the black.

'That's Arabic writing. That,' Mum pointed, 'presumably means snail.'

'Are you going to learn to read in Arabic?' I asked Bea in amazement.

'Yes,' she said. 'I already know that you have to start from the right of the page.'

I bowed my head. I wished I knew what side that was.

'Look, there's a picture of a girl with blonde hair.' I leafed through for an orange one. 'Why are all the people dressed in English clothes?' There was one picture of a boy in a djellaba and a round cap but he was a shepherd and he wasn't at school. He was on a mountain like Abdul, surrounded by sheep.

As soon as Bea's clothes were ready she started school. My heart was swollen with envy and pride and fear for her. Mum, Linda, Mob and I watched her set off, hand in hand with Ayesha, her stiff white clothes standing out around her like wrapping. Even Ayesha's grandmother gave us a smile as she shook her rugs into the courtyard.

'My nappies,' Linda suddenly shrieked. 'My nappies have gone. I hung them out last night. Five nappies and a vest.'

'Here's the vest,' I said. It was still hanging on the railing. 'It's dry.'

'Maybe they fell into the courtyard,' Mum suggested.

Linda was already heading for the stairs.

'They're not here,' she bawled up a minute later, drawing several people out on to the landing. 'Has anyone seen NAPPIES?' Linda shouted to them.

'NAPPIES?' She drew a square in the air with her hands.

I crouched in the doorway. Icy with embarrassment. The Henna Ladies had come out and were watching from their landing. They waved at me.

I heaved Mob up in my arms and took her inside as my excuse.

'You don't mind, do you?' I looked down into her pale blue eyes. 'About nappy thieves?'

Mob and I sat side by side on the mattress that was now my and Bea's bed and listened to the high-pitched shrieks and bitter explanations as Linda interrogated one after another of the inhabitants of the hotel.

'When we go out can I carry Mob on my back like the girls in the square?'

Linda was still distracted over her loss.

'You know Khadija? And the beggar girls in the Djemaa El Fna?'

'Yes,' Linda said.

'Well, they carry their baby brothers and sisters around on their backs. They tie them on with a piece of material. We could use a bedspread.'

Linda was counting through her pile of remaining 47

nappies in varying shades of grey and white. 'All right, if you really want to,' she agreed.

A bell was being rung as we waited at the gates of Bea's school. Children began to appear.

I pulled out the bedspread. 'Will you tie her on now?'

I stood with my feet squarely apart to keep from being toppled over by the wriggling weight. Mob's damp towelling body pressed against my back as she was knotted tightly on, over one shoulder and across my chest. I sweated to think of Khadija gliding through the crowds, her bundle of baby borne lightly as a shawl. I longed to sit down.

At that perfect moment Bea appeared. I took a few unsteady steps towards her. Mob began to yell and pull my hair.

'Bea! Yoo-hoo!' Mum and Linda waved and called to attract her attention.

My legs were beginning to shiver with the strain. Bea took one look at me and I heard like a prayer, 'Can I have a go?'

I twisted up my mouth and paused for as long as I could bear. 'Seeing as it's your first day . . .' I said, and I sat down heavily and too fast and began fumbling with the knot.

Mob was transferred to Bea's back and we set off for lunch in the square. I watched her face for signs of strain, and was soon rewarded by a definite loss of colour, a breathy voice, dawdling behind, and 'She's quite heavy, isn't she?'

There was a burst of laughter. 'Well, you lasted five minutes longer than your sister.' Linda tweaked her cheek. 'She's not been fed on Heinz baby food for nothing.'

As we dipped bread into the circles of olive oil that floated on our scalding bowls of soup, Bea told about her day.

'We sat in a room and copied everything the teacher said. One girl got beaten with a stick.'

Mum was horrified. 'Why?'

'Because she peed in the classroom. The teacher beat her until the stick broke, and then when the stick broke everyone was very happy, and then a boy from the school next door who is her favourite boy brought over a new stick.'

'My God.' Mum put her head in her hands.

'Are you going to go again tomorrow?' I asked.

'Of course.' Bea was adamant.

'Linda had five nappies stolen.' I wanted her to 49

know what she'd missed. 'Mum thinks it might be the Henna Ladies.'

'No, I do not. They probably just blew away.'

Linda muttered under her breath and fed Mob another piece of bread. 'Prostitutes,' she hissed.

Each morning I dressed in my black trousers and tucked my hair up into a hat. I was keeping watch for Bilal. I waited in the courtyard, amusing myself by walking along the white lines between the tiles, precariously balancing, one foot in front of the other, as if it were a tightrope. I was also on the lookout for stray nappies. Every day, whatever time of day or night Linda hung out her washing, when she came to take it in, at least one nappy would be missing. I was sure I had seen one of the Henna Ladies coming out of the downstairs toilet wearing one on her head like a turban. So far not one had been recovered.

'If things carry on like this I shall have to think of going home,' Linda said more than once.

I woke to the pounding on wood of feet and fists, and the screaming voice of a woman. I jumped up. Linda was not in her bed. Mum sat up sleepily, but on hearing the roar that was beginning to build outside, she sprang up and rushed out in her nightie. I watched her race round to where Linda was hammering. She was beating on the closed door of the Henna Ladies – the Nappy Thieves. She was shouting for them to come out. Ayesha's grandmother hobbled out on to the landing. She stumbled to help drag Linda away. Linda clung, swearing, to the railings, and then the door opened and the two women stepped out, draped in bright silk, their hair loose.

'Quick, Bea, come and look,' I screamed.

The gallery was a flurry of cloth and hair and the woman from our left whose cushion had been ruined was hurling slippers at my mother's head. Slippers, fruit, anything she could find. Her husband stood in the doorway and shouted. I looked over the railings for Moulay Idriss to come out of his little room but he was not at home. Mum picked up an orange that rolled along the landing. She held it in her strong hand and flung it back, hitting the cushion woman on the ear with a smack so ferocious that for a moment everything else was quiet.

I dragged on my trousers and ran round along the other side of the landing. I wanted to pull at the skirt of my mother's nightdress and force her back into our room. I wanted her to be still and calm and never go out again. As I ran I slipped and fell, scraping my knee across the stone floor. I curled up on the ground and stared into the jagged cut across my trouser leg. Inside a graze was filling up with blood. I sobbed. Now Bilal would never see my trousers with a zip. I pulled myself up, blind with pity, my forehead swelling to a bruise. I headed for home, forgetting.

There was Mum, dragging the stove from John's broken-down van. She was dragging it through the door. Dragging it with her along the landing. The people shrank away. She was trying to lift it. Throw it. Finally she hurled it. Her hands bleeding. It bounced and scraped along the landing, forcing people back into doorways. She followed in its wake. The blood from her fingers running down her arms. 'Stop it! Stop it!' I could hear myself screaming as if it were someone else's voice. Bea was behind me shouting in Arabic. The metal of the stove still clanked and smashed against the railings.

A hand on my shoulder made me turn and a woman's arm drew me through a doorway into a lamplit room. Bea and I crouched behind a mound of cushions under a wall thick with hangings. The room was heavy with the clamour of outside and the woman stood in the middle of the room, anxiously watching the door. She was young and beautiful, dressed in a 53 caftan threaded with gold. I had seen her husband, a rich man, waiting his turn to use the toilet by the stairs.

'They want to find out how the poor people live,' Ayesha had told us. 'They have a big house with servants. But now they live here.'

The woman looked at us with gentle eyes. She knelt down and touched the fraying edges of my trousers.

'Take them off,' Bea nudged, in response to the woman's murmurings.

My ears were full of the pounding of the fight behind the door. The echo of it rose and fell in waves. She pulled me up and began carefully to peel away my precious trousers, lifting each foot as she slipped them off. I did nothing to help. She sat me on a stool and washed the cut with water and a soft cloth. She smeared it with bright red cream that looked like blood. I smiled at the gore of it.

'Come through,' she said with her eyes. Bea and I followed her into a smaller room. A baby was sleeping on a bed piled high with cushions, on to which we climbed. From this windowless room only the occasional shout drifted in from outside. The lady brought us glasses of milk and coils of bright orange pastry filled with honey, so sweet it stung your mouth.

I lay back on the bed and closed my eyes, flickering my lids against a haunting of my mother's bleeding hands.

I was being carried through bright sunlight. I struggled against strong unfamiliar arms.

'Put me down.' I kicked, and a dark face swam into my vision. Smiling at me.

'Bilal.' I clung to him, my arms twisting round his neck. We were on the landing outside our room. A quiet lunchtime breeze murmured through the hotel – the smell of food behind closed doors. My mother was walking just behind, holding Bea by the hand and carrying my trousers in the other.

'Good afternoon,' she said, as if by chance she hadn't seen me for a long time.

PENGUIN 60s

READ MORE IN PENGUIN

For complete information about books available from Penguin and how to order them, please write to us at the appropriate address below. Please note that for copyright reasons the selection of books varies from country to country.

IN THE UNITED KINGDOM: Please write to *Dept. EP, Penguin Books Ltd, Bath Road, Harmondsworth, Middlesex UB7 0DA.*

IN THE UNITED STATES: Please write to *Consumer Sales, Penguin USA, P.O. Box 999, Dept. 17109, Bergenfield, New Jersey 07621-0120.* VISA and MasterCard holders call 1-800-253-6476 to order Penguin titles.

IN CANADA: Please write to *Penguin Books Canada Ltd, 10 Alcorn Avenue, Suite 300, Toronto, Ontario M4V 3B2.*

IN AUSTRALIA: Please write to *Penguin Books Australia Ltd, P.O. Box 257, Ringwood, Victoria 3134.*

IN NEW ZEALAND: Please write to *Penguin Books (NZ) Ltd, Private Bag 102902, North Shore Mail Centre, Auckland 10.*

IN INDIA: Please write to *Penguin Books India Pvt Ltd, 706 Eros Apartments, 56 Nehru Place, New Delhi 110 019.*

IN THE NETHERLANDS: Please write to *Penguin Books Netherlands bv, Postbus 3507, NL-1001 AH Amsterdam.*

IN GERMANY: Please write to *Penguin Books Deutschland GmbH, Metzlerstrasse 26, 60594 Frankfurt am Main.*

IN SPAIN: Please write to *Penguin Books S. A., Bravo Murillo 19, 1° B, 28015 Madrid.*

IN ITALY: Please write to *Penguin Italia s.r.l., Via Felice Casati 20, I-20124 Milano.*

IN FRANCE: Please write to *Penguin France S. A., 17 rue Lejeune, F-31000 Toulouse.*

IN JAPAN: Please write to *Penguin Books Japan, Ishikiribashi Building, 2-5-4, Suido, Bunkyo-ku, Tokyo 112.*

IN GREECE: Please write to *Penguin Hellas Ltd, Dimocritou 3, GR-106 71 Athens.*

IN SOUTH AFRICA: Please write to *Longman Penguin Southern Africa (Pty) Ltd, Private Bag X08, Bertsham 2013.*